# The Magical Lives
## The Power of Having Faith

"New beginnings are often disguised as painful endings." Lao Tzu

Created by Alexandra Angheluta
Illustrated by Polina Hrytskova

Printed in the United States of America
First Printing, 2019
ISBN: 9781793095114
Library of Congress Control Number: 2019908355

Independently published by PlaySitters Hawaii
www.PlaySittersHawaii.com

With her sparkly cinnamon skin,
And her chocolate hair tied loosely in a pin
Liv was feeling so much happiness radiating from within.

But then,
Her head really started to spin!

"I live in a place where every day is the same,
And though this place is filled with warm summer rain,
The problem is,
Life feels too tame."

Liv began to walk, she walked for a while.
She believes it had to be more than a mile!
Finally, when she couldn't walk anymore,
Lo and behold, she came upon a door.

Liv didn't know what to do!
She felt fear!
And excitement too!

"On the other side of the door is a new kind of life
But how do I know, it's not filled with strife?"

Liv decided
she had no choice.
She had to listen to her
intuition,

That inside voice.

"I am safe.
It is only change.
New experiences make my
life wonderful.
Even if at first it feels strange."

Her mind whispered,
"Your faith will pull you through!"

And her heart faintly sang
"Adieu, adieu, adieu."

Liv chose faith and opened that door.
She had come upon something she had never seen before.
This is the first time that she had left that seashore.

There were leaves:
All up her sleeves!
All because Liv chose to Believe!

Reds, oranges and yellows!
It wasn't just sand and sun that helped Liv feel mellow!
Even though this new place was not as bright,
There still was so much beauty in sight.

There was a feeling of letting the old go:
Of anything that was causing her to feel any woe.

She jumped and jumped
on those piles of leaves and her mind shouted:

"Anything can happen if you just believe!"

But then, the unthinkable happened when that last leaf dropped.

Liv's heart just kinda... flopped.

She looked around, there was no sun. And the leaves on the trees, now there were none.

Liv just realized, this is not so fun.

With her heart full of worry,
and her mind in a blurry,
Liv had a feeling she should get out of there, and hurry.

Her mind kept whispering,
"Your faith will pull you through!"

And her heart faintly sang
"Adieu, adieu, adieu."

She ran and ran through the colors of autumn

Until Liv felt herself fall straight on her bottom!

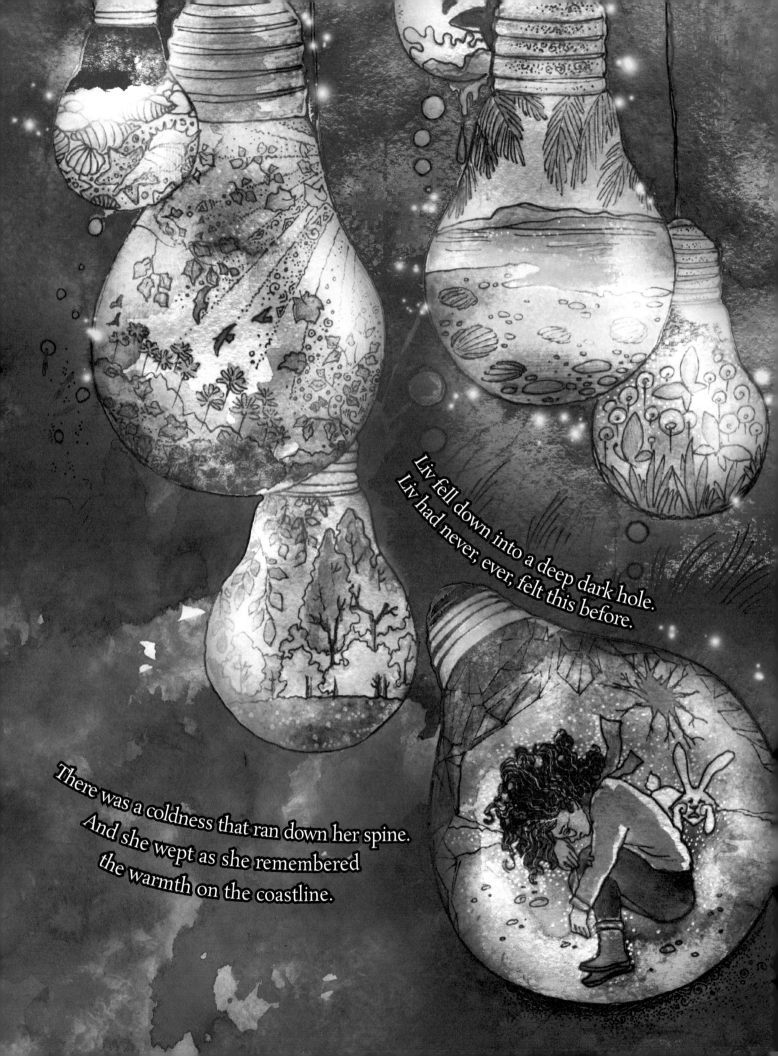

Liv fell down into a deep dark hole.
Liv had never, ever, felt this before.

There was a coldness that ran down her spine.
And she wept as she remembered
the warmth on the coastline.

This time, Liv could not see
any beauty about.
There was only darkness,
and she was full of fear and doubt.

She felt stuck in that lightless hole.
However, that was where Liv was
able to hear the voice of her soul.

Liv came upon an important realization,
As she sat there in a quiet meditation.
All that she needed came from within,
It didn't matter if her surroundings were sunny or dim.
She was born to experience both.
And adventures such as these will lead to her growth.

Liv then repeated these words with the strongest faith:

"I open new doors to life,
I know I am always safe,
I am willing to change and grow!"

Her mind kept repeating,
"Your faith will pull you through"

And her heart faintly sang, "Adieu, adieu, adieu."

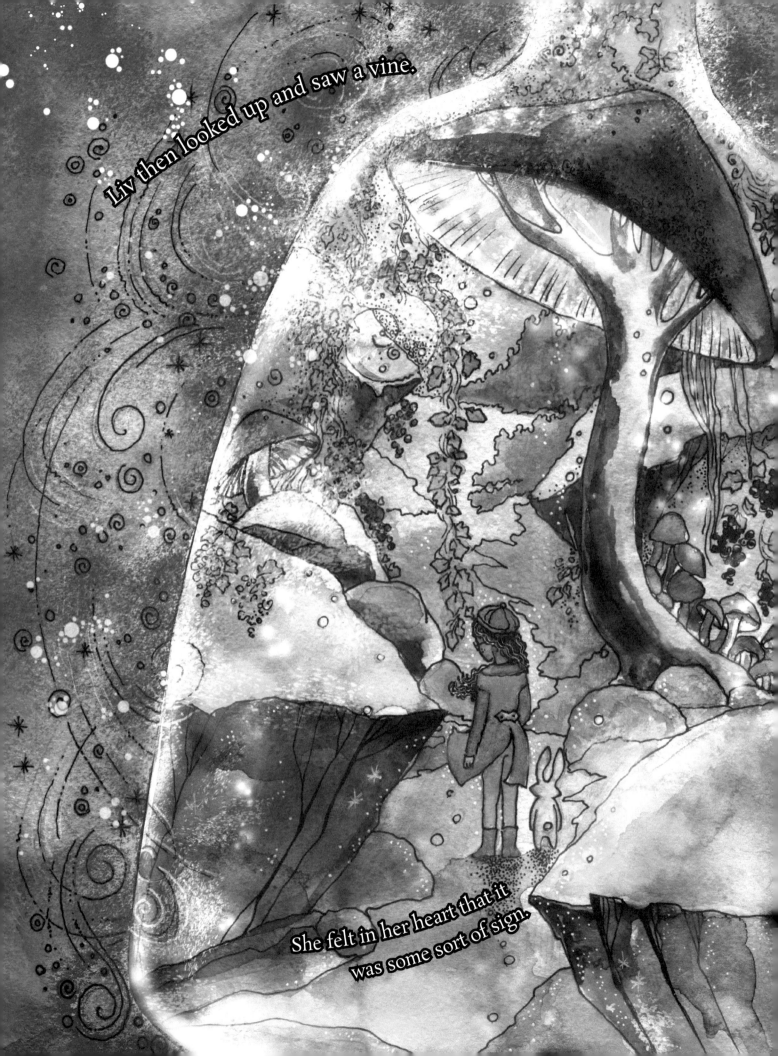

Liv then looked up and saw a vine.

She felt in her heart that it was some sort of sign.

When Liv climbed out, there was a white glow all around.
She felt so delighted to lay upon the snow on the ground.

She spread her arms that now felt like wings
And yelled to the sky, "I am ready for all that life brings!"

And even though her skin felt so cold, this was the warmest Liv had ever felt, as if she was full of gold.

For she finally knew, her faith will always pull her through.,

She watched the snowflakes drop silently around her,
And felt at peace surrounded in the quiet of nature.

The majestic alpine firs let out a whisper
That everything always comes to an end, even winter.

As the snow disappeared,
Liv felt that her mixture of feelings had finally cleared!
She accepted that endings will always be due,
To make space for something new.

And this is when Liv saw it,
Another entrance she can pass through.
Her mind excitedly shouted,
"Your faith pulled you through!"
And her heart faintly sang
"Adieu, adieu, adieu."

She leaped for joy and felt a thrill,
When there in the distance was
the most beautiful hill!

And that's when she knew:
Environments change
Feelings change
We change.

She took a breath
and then a step,

Oh the beautiful
things she saw
with every footstep.

She felt grateful for all of the
possibilities of life, of starting anew.

Even for those seasons that
will cause her to feel blue!

Liv learned that everything she wants
is on the other side of fear.
And that is when she decided to take
herself right out of that sphere.

Her mind kept repeating
"Your faith will pull you through"
And her heart faintly sang
"Adieu, adieu, adieu."

Liv found herself in a new kind of space. She was sure that she was no longer contained in a vase!

This new environment was full of grace. She couldn't explain the feeling, that she came from this place.

And just like that,
Liv felt like
she was fully embraced.

# Affirmations for Change

We can teach affirmations to children to help improve their well being. Affirmations can help boost self-confidence and create a positive mindset. Practice these positive affirmations with your children daily! They will become a part of their inner voice and will help them during times of challenging emotions.

I am loved.

I am connected to all of life.

I am brave.

I open new doors to life. I know I am always safe. I am willing to change and grow.

I am safe. It is only change. Love surrounds me.

My life gets better all the time with wonderful new experiences.

I face this challenge with strength and I know I will get through this.

I embrace this season of my life.

I am open to infinite possibilities.

I am willing to step into the unknown.

This book is dedicated to the women authors who have helped strengthen my faith in the Universe.

A special thanks to Louise Hay.

# About the Author

Alexandra C. Angheluta has been connecting with children for years through her business, PlaySitters Hawaii: Using the Educational and Therapeutical Value of Play. Through her work and her educational background in social work and play therapy, Alexandra saw the need for more material to help children through challenging times in their lives. Her Magical Affirmations books focus on teaching children how to heal from within on topics focused around emotional growth. Alexandra is also the author of *The Magical Gray Flower: The Power of Self-Love*. She now resides in Portland, Oregon where she continues to engage with children in the magical world of play.

Thank you for your purchase! If you enjoyed this book, please leave a review on Amazon. You can follow Alexandra @magical_affirmations to stay updated on new releases, including her new book *The Magical Dreamcatcher: The Power of Believing In Your Inner Light*.

"Always believe that something wonderful is about to happen." - Dr. Sukhraj Dhillon

25948895R00024